Aus

The Two Gorillas

Becky's two gorillas lived inside
her doll's house. One was green
and the other was red.
They were very scary gorillas
until Becky gave them their
first bath.

Which Aussie Nibbles have you read?

Aussie Nibbles

The Two Gorillas

Ursula Dubosarsky

Illustrated by Mitch Vane

Puffin Books

Puffin Books
Penguin Books Australia Ltd
487 Maroondah Highway, PO Box 257
Ringwood, Victoria 3134, Australia
Penguin Books Ltd
Harmondsworth, Middlesex, England
Penguin Putnam Inc.
375 Hudson Street, New York, New York 10014, USA
Penguin Books Canada Limited
10 Alcorn Avenue, Toronto, Ontario, Canada, M4V 3B2
Penguin Books (N.Z.) Ltd
Cnr Rosedale and Airborne Roads, Albany, Auckland, New Zealand
Penguin Books (South Africa) (Pty) Ltd
24 Sturdee Avenue, Rosebank, Johannesburg 2196, South Africa
Penguin Books India (P) Ltd
11, Community Centre, Panchsheel Park, New Delhi 110 017, India

First published by Penguin Books Australia, 2000

3 5 7 9 10 8 6 4

Typeset in New Century School Book by Post Pre-press Group,
Brisbane, Queensland
Printed and bound in Australia by McPherson's Printing Group,
Maryborough, Victoria

Designed by Melissa Fraser, Penguin Design Studio
Series editor: Kay Ronai

National Library of Australia
Cataloguing-in-Publication data:
Dubosarsky, Ursula, 1961– .
The two gorillas.
ISBN 0 14 130796 X.
I. Vane, Mitch. II. Title. (Series: Aussie nibbles).
A823.3

www.puffin.com.au

For Simon and Leo, my dear little
nephews in Tasmania. *U.D.*

For my brave mum. *M.V.*

Chapter One

Inside Becky's doll's house
were two gorillas.

One was green and the
other one was red. They
were best friends.

In the daytime, they sat

on the little sofa in the
living room of the doll's
house and watched
television.

In the night-time they

lay down flat in bed, if
Becky remembered to put
them there. If she forgot,
they stayed up watching
television all night.

The two gorillas didn't
say much.

They didn't say 'Good
morning' or 'How are you?'
They just said 'Grrrrrrrrrrrr.'

'Grrrrrrr,' said the red gorilla.

'Grrrrrrr,' said the green gorilla.

They were very scary.

Chapter Two

One day, Becky decided it
was time to give the two
gorillas a bath.

'You have to sit still,' she
told them, 'while I put you
in the sink. If you wiggle,

I will bite you.'

She showed them her
teeth. They did look sharp.

'Grrrrrrrr,' said the red
gorilla.

'Grrrrrrrr,' said the green
gorilla.

Becky filled the sink with
water and she even put in
some bubble bath.

When there were lots of
bubbles, she put the
gorillas in too.

They sank right down
to the bottom.

'That's funny,' said Becky.
'I thought you would float.'

The gorillas couldn't say
anything because their
mouths were full of water.

Glug. Glug. Glug.

Chapter Three

When Becky pulled the two
gorillas out of their bath,
they were very clean.

They were so clean,
in fact, they were white.
The bath had washed all

their colour off.

'Grrrrrrrrrr,' said the
white gorilla.

'Grrrrrrrrrr,' said the
other white gorilla.

Becky frowned.

'I know,' she said, after thinking a moment. 'I will colour you in.'

She went over to her

texta box. Becky had
hundreds and hundreds
of textas. Well, she had
hundreds and hundreds
of textas, but only one
that worked.

It was pink.

Becky coloured in the two
gorillas with the pink texta.
Now she had two pink
gorillas.

'Grrrrrrrr,' said the two

pink gorillas together.

Becky shook her head.

'I can't tell which is which,'
she said. 'I will have to
decorate one of you.'

She picked up one of the

gorillas and took him over
to her craft box. She covered
him with glue and then she
sprinkled silver and gold
glitter all over him so you
couldn't see his face.

'Eurgh!' said Becky. 'You look awful.'

So she put him in the cupboard inside the doll's house and shut the door.

The pink gorilla sat on the sofa and watched television all by himself.

Chapter Four

Next morning, Becky
opened the cupboard and
took out the ugly gorilla.
She peered at him closely.

'You don't look very well,
gorilla,' she said. 'In fact,

I think you are dead. Time
for your funeral.'

Becky took the two
gorillas out into the garden.

In one corner, she saw
a big pile of dirt.

'That'll do,' she said.

She dug a hole in the
dirt and put the dead
gorilla inside it. Then she

covered him with pebbles.
The pink gorilla helped.
Becky sang a little dead
gorilla song.

'Grrrrrrrrrrr,' said the
pink gorilla.

The other gorilla didn't
say anything because he
was dead now.

Becky took the pink
gorilla back inside and put
him in the doll's house.

He looked tired, so she
laid him on the bed.
He stared at the ceiling.

Chapter Five

The next day when Becky
woke up in the morning,
she looked straight over
at the pink gorilla. He was
lying there, doing nothing.

'I wonder what happens

when you freeze a gorilla,'
thought Becky.

She jumped out of bed.
She picked up the pink

gorilla and took him into
the kitchen.

She got out some plastic
and wrapped him up, round
and round. He looked like a
mummy.

'Now!' said Becky.

She stood up on her toes
and pushed him into the
freezer, underneath a bag of
frozen peas.

Chapter Six

Now there were no gorillas
in the doll's house.

Without the gorillas, it
didn't really look like a
doll's house. It just looked
like a bookshelf.

In a few days, it was
filled with books.

In a few more days it was
also covered with toys and
clothes and cups and bits of
paper.

Becky forgot it had ever
been a doll's house.

She even forgot about the
two gorillas.

Chapter Seven

It was a hot, hot day.

'Ice cream!' shouted Becky's baby brother from the floor. 'Ice cream!!'

He ran over to the fridge and stood up on a chair.

He reached into the freezer and grabbed the frozen gorilla. He pulled off the plastic and put the gorilla in his mouth.

Becky's little brother was
very happy. He thought the
frozen gorilla was delicious.
That afternoon, Becky
felt a strange lump under

the carpet. She bent down
and pulled it out.

'Oh,' said Becky.

The gorilla! He wasn't
pink any more. And he had

some bits missing. Arms
and legs and things like
that. But he was still a
gorilla.

'Poor gorilla,' said Becky. 'I'm sorry. I forgot all about you.'

'Grrrr,' said the gorilla with the bits missing.

Chapter Eight

Becky took the gorilla to
her room. She went over
to the bookshelf that used
to be a doll's house and
tipped all the books and toys
and things onto the floor.

She found the little sofa
and the television and the
bed. She set them all up in
the right place.

She sat the gorilla on the

sofa in front of the television.

'Glad to be back, gorilla?'
said Becky.

'Grrrrrrrrrr,' said the
gorilla in a funny voice.

He sounded so soft.

So soft.

Becky looked at him for a moment.

'Are you lonely, gorilla?' asked Becky.

Chapter Nine

Becky went out into the garden. She picked up her spade and walked over to where she had buried the dead gorilla.

She dug and she dug and

she dug. And she dug.

It took a long time, but at
last she found him. He was
grimy and slimy and
glittery but he was still
a gorilla.

'Gorilla!' said Becky. 'Are
you all right?'

She took a deep breath.

She breathed into his

mouth with lots of puffs.

Puff, puff, puff.

'I think you're looking
better, gorilla,' she said
after a while. 'In fact,
I think you're alive again!'
    'Grrrrrrrr,' said the dirty
gorilla.

Chapter Ten

Becky went back inside
with the dirty gorilla. She
put him on the sofa with
the other gorilla.

She stared at them. They
should be happy now.

But were they?

'There's something
wrong,' said Becky, shaking
her head, thinking hard.
'Hmmmmm.'

She went over to her

craft box and got out her
scissors. Then she picked
up the dirty gorilla.

'I hope this doesn't hurt,
gorilla,' she said.

She cut off one of his

arms. Then she cut off
one of his legs. Then she
stuck the leg and the arm
on the other gorilla with
sticky tape.

'That's better,' said Becky,
pleased. 'Now you're the
same!'

She put the two gorillas
back on the sofa. They sat
there together in front of
the television, each with
one arm and one leg.

They did look better.
They even looked as though
they might be smiling.

'Perfect,' said Becky.

And this time, the two
gorillas didn't say anything
at all.

They didn't have to.

They were perfect.

Two perfectly happy

gorillas.

From Ursula Dubosarsky

For my sixth birthday my mum and
dad gave me a furry toy koala.
I loved him so much I used to eat
him. I ate off all his black plastic
claws and I ate the fur off his ears.

Then he looked so sad I felt sorry
for him, so I got a texta and drew
a little smile under his black nose.
He looked sadder than ever!
Maybe thinking about him helped
me write this story.

From Mitch Vane

As soon as I read *The Two Gorillas*
I was itching to get my sketch book
out. I love gorillas.

This book brought back very fond
childhood memories. Nearly all of
my toys suffered a similar fate as
the two gorillas – usually with the
use of a blunt pair of scissors and
a very permanent biro.

Aussie Nibbles

Fairy Bread

Ursula Dubosarsky

Illustrated by Mitch Vane

Becky only wants fairy bread at
her party. But there's so much left
over, and she won't throw it out.

Aussie Nibbles

Follow That Lion!

Rosemary Hayes

Illustrated by Stephen Michael King

Hector's mum has found an
unusual pet. She says it is gentle.
Hector knows better . . .

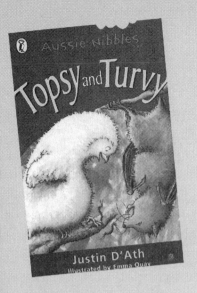

Why are Topsy and Turvy
so different?
One day they learn why.

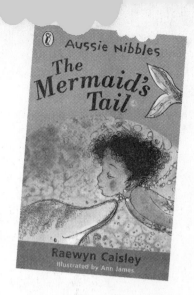

Crystal longs to be a
mermaid. So her mother
makes her a special tail.

It is Kerry's first day
at her new school.
Will she find a friend?

It's Saturday morning. Auskick
is about to start. But Brendan
thinks his pet fish is sick.

Hector's mum has found an
unusual pet. She says it is gentle.
Hector knows better . . .

Becky only wants fairy bread at
her party. But there's so much left
over, and she won't throw it out.

Their grandmother loved blue.
She also hated her grey hair.
Sonya and Margo knew what to do.

Benny loves the dog that
lives nearby.
But why is it so sad?